Petrouchka

THE STORY OF THE BALLET

ILLUSTRATED BY
JOHN COLLIER

RETOLD BY
VIVIAN WERNER

LONDON · VICTOR GOLLANCZ LTD · 1992

INTRODUCTION

All over the world, children love Punch and Judy, though they may call the puppets by different names. In France, for instance, Punch is known as Guignol. In Italy, sometimes he is Pedralino and sometimes Pagliacci. In Russia, he's called Petrouchka (Pə·troosh·kä), and his story is told in the ballet set to the music of the Russian composer Igor Stravinsky.

Stravinsky wrote the ballet in 1910 and 1911 for his friend Sergei Diaghilev, who was the impresario, or manager, of a ballet company called the Ballets Russes, or Russian Ballet. Diaghilev took care of all artistic and financial matters, including hiring and paying workers, composers, dancers, and designers.

For *Petrouchka*, Diaghilev asked his Russian friend Alexandre Benois to design the scenery and costumes. He chose Michel Fokine to choreograph the dances, the French conductor Pierre Monteux to lead the musicians, and Vaslav Nijinsky, perhaps the greatest dancer of all time, to dance the role of Petrouchka.

Diaghilev, Stravinsky, and Benois drew on their memories of the Butter Week fairs in

St Petersburg—the fairs that took place just before Lent—to work out the story of Petrouchka. There were always puppet shows at those fairs, and Petrouchka was usually the main character. He was an unpleasant fellow who beat his wife, killed people, and was finally carried off to Hell by the Devil. Between the acts of the puppet shows, two characters appeared before the closed curtains. Their faces were painted black, and they had wide, white painted mouths. They amused the crowd by hitting each other over the head with sticks.

Of course, the three Russian men didn't simply copy the puppet drama for their ballet; they made important changes. The ballet would be about the puppet Petrouchka, but in a symbolic way it would also be about the turmoil in Russia, their homeland, and about the problems of being a human being. Petrouchka would no longer be a bully. Instead, he would be a brokenhearted clown, a complicated character. And the two figures in blackface would be replaced by one, the Moor, who would become a more central character in the drama. Rather than beating his wife, Petrouchka would beat his head against the wall in frustration when the Moor wins the love of a beautiful Ballerina. And instead of being carried off by the Devil, Petrouchka would be tortured by the demons of his own thoughts.

The setting of *Petrouchka* was to be as close to the real fair at St Petersburg as possible. Even the travelling showman who introduced the puppets to the crowd at the real fair was included as a main player. And as Benois sketched the designs for the scenery, he remembered exactly the way the fair booths had looked—the booth where *blini* were sold, the booth where gingerbread was sold, the booth where tea was served. He even found a real carousel to put on the stage!

Petrouchka was first performed in Paris on June 13, 1911, by the Ballets Russes. It was a great success. Since then it has been performed all over the world and by many companies. The choreography is not always the same, though. Sometimes, too, the scenery and costumes are different. But no matter where or how *Petrouchka* is performed, everyone is touched by the story of the little puppet with a heart and soul, the one who longed to catch a snowflake on his tongue, who longed to smell a flower. That Petrouchka will live forever.

—V.W.

It was Shrove Tuesday, the day of the annual Shrovetide Fair, and the people of old St Petersburg were in a festive mood. They gathered in the town square, laughing and joking, waving and shouting greetings to one another, slapping one another on the back.

They all knew that Lent would begin the very next day. There would be no feasting after that—no dancing, no merry-making at all until Easter, many long weeks away.

Snow floated down in feathery flakes on that Shrove Tuesday, over a hundred and fifty years ago. It settled alike on the kerchiefed heads of peasant women and the elegant coats of gentlemen. It drifted over the graceful yellow and pink and pale blue buildings that ringed the square, and coated the colourfully decorated booths inside it.

Early as it was, those scarlet and green and gold booths had been set up even earlier. Now the old women bustled about, busily setting out their wares. Shivering, they pulled their fringed shawls closer around their shoulders to ward off the cold.

One pudgy little woman in a long, bright apron festooned her booth with fat ropes of sausage. Another polished the big brass samovar in which she would brew her fragrant tea. Still another poked at a pile of coals in the brass box of a brazier, coaxing them into flame. Later she would cook tiny pancakes that were called *blini* over the fire.

4

A group of peasants had arrived early. They wore feast-day clothes, bright tunics embroidered in every colour of the rainbow. Underneath were black trousers tucked into tall black boots. Trying to warm themselves, the peasants stamped their feet and flapped their arms like chickens.

At the sight of their first customers, the women in the booths turned to the business at hand. One passed around glasses of steaming tea from her samovar, pocketing the kopecks the peasants handed her. One hacked off huge hunks of sausage and handed them to the hungry men. One flipped her golden brown *blini* onto plates and spooned sour cream over them.

Before long a swarm of Gypsies whirled into view, dancing and clapping their hands or shaking tambourines. Rows of gold bracelets on their bare arms jingled and clanked as they roamed about, selling trinkets or reading palms.

All eyes were on the Gypsies until a group of noblemen turned into the square. They were dressed in long, black, fur-trimmed greatcoats that showed off their handsome figures. While the Gypsies danced and sang, the nobles strutted about as if they owned the world.

More and more people thronged into the square, jostling and bumping and elbowing one another. Shouting at the tops of their lungs, pedlars hawked their goods from trays that hung from their shoulders: whistles and carved wooden dolls, lemon drops and candy sticks, golden brown gingerbread baked in such fantastic shapes as flying birds and flying horses and splendid castles with flying flags.

As the crowd grew, the excitement rose. A merry-go-round turned and turned. A hurdy-gurdy played while young girls danced to its sad, thin tune.

The noise and the din and the swirl of the crowd created a feeling of celebration everywhere. Everywhere, that is, but at the far end of the square, where a lone booth stood with its curtains closed. This booth was larger than the rest and far more elaborately decorated. A big, bright sign was stretched along one side. Written on the sign, in a large, curious script, were the words *Living Theatre.*

At first all was silent, almost eerie, around the theatre. Finally, though, two drummers appeared and beat out a rat-a-tat-tat that rang through the square. When its echoes had died out, the drummers stepped aside. The crowd turned their heads as the curtains parted just enough to let a strange old man step forward. He wore a long black wizard's robe and a high-peaked wizard's hat.

The Old Magician stood watching the crowd. A crafty smile twitched his thin lips, and an evil gleam lit his eye. Suddenly, he flung his arms out in a wide, sweeping gesture, and a hush fell over all. Something wonderful was about to happen.

As the Old Magician stepped into the square, he drew forth a flute and began to play a mournful, haunting tune. With the first few notes, the curtains flew open. And there stood three life-size puppets, each in its own little compartment.

The dainty Ballerina was in the centre. She looked like a china doll, with long eyelashes, a mouth painted bright crimson, and vivid spots of red on her cheeks. She was beautiful, and she held her head high as if waiting to be admired.

On one side of the Ballerina was the powerful Moor. He wore a shimmering turban and brilliant blue robes. He was as pleased with his appearance as the Ballerina was with hers.

On the other side of the Ballerina stood the pathetic Petrouchka. His body was as limp as a handkerchief. Loose trousers drooped over his boots, and his blouse had a row of ridiculous ruffles at the neck. It was a peculiar costume, suitable only for a clown.

Everyone laughed at the awkward puppet. The sound wounded Petrouchka, and he put his hand over his heart, as if that could ease his pain. But it only grew worse, and he wanted to weep.

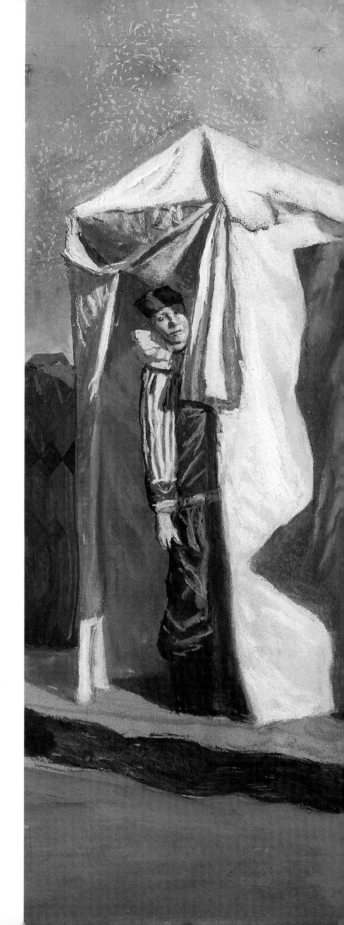

If only they knew he had a heart, Petrouchka thought, these people wouldn't laugh at him. Or if they knew he had a soul, or if he could tell them of his dreams, his yearnings. Petrouchka longed to smell flowers, to catch snowflakes on his tongue, to feel the biting cold. He longed to dance. To dance when he felt like it, not when he was ordered to.

Just then, the Old Magician blew on his flute. The Ballerina obeyed the command to dance at once; the Moor obeyed almost as quickly. Finally, even the reluctant Petrouchka knew he had no choice.

The dolls' arms and legs were stiff and awkward as they danced, and their heads jerked from side to side as if pulled by strings. But there were no strings. The magician's music made the puppets move.

"Look," the onlookers cried, delighted with the spectacle. "Look! The puppets are dancing!" The crowd was ecstatic when the three puppets stepped out into the square. People clapped and shouted and cheered. But the one they applauded loudest was the beautiful Ballerina.

Their applause deeply touched Petrouchka, for he himself was in love with the Ballerina. He wished he were brave enough to tell her so! What if she had a heart and a soul, too? Perhaps she even loved *him*. . . . The thought whirled around in Petrouchka's head like the snowflakes whirling in the square. Like them, the idea sent chills through and through him. *If she loves me,* he thought, . . . *loves me . . . loves me. . . .*

He danced closer to the Ballerina, but she was absorbed by the exotic Moor and the antics of the crowd. When Petrouchka was almost at the Ballerina's side, he held one hand over his heart and reached the other out to her.

"I love you," he was telling her. "I love you!"

But the Ballerina jumped back, frightened. Petrouchka was so strange, she thought. So awkward, too. And, really, he was only a clown!

But Petrouchka was not the only one smitten with the Ballerina. The Moor had been watching the others out of the corner of his eye, and now he saw his chance. Gliding to the Ballerina's side, he began to flirt with her. She was happy, but Petrouchka was heartsick. Terrible pangs of jealousy made him so angry that he trembled with rage.

Meanwhile, the crowd in the square was enthralled. They could sense that the puppets had almost turned into living and feeling human beings!

Petrouchka did not notice the crowd. He could think only of the Ballerina and the Moor. So when he saw a large stick lying on the ground, he picked it up and shook it in the Moor's face. The Moor merely stared at Petrouchka with the utmost contempt until the sorry little clown trembled with fear rather than rage. Terrified, he turned and fled.

The Moor followed, but before he could catch up, Petrouchka stumbled and fell. The crowd watched, spellbound, as the Moor planted one foot on the little puppet's back, pinning him down.

The Old Magician didn't like what he saw at all. Why must Petrouchka cause such a fuss? After all, he was only a doll, the Magician's creation. Didn't he understand that? At the sound of three sharp notes on the flute, Petrouchka got to his feet, and all three puppets began to dance stiffly.

Soon the crowd was bored by this forced dancing, and most of them wandered off. Then the Old Magician ordered the Moor and the Ballerina to their rooms, and he himself dragged Petrouchka off to his shabby little cell.

Petrouchka's cell was tiny and bare, without a stick of furniture. Petrouchka hated it more than anything in the world.

He hated the clouds painted near the ceiling; he hated the painted mountain peaks, which only made him think of the great wide world beyond. He hated the demons and dragons drawn all around, a sign that he was doomed to suffer here forever. Most of all, Petrouchka hated the dark and shadowy portrait of the Old Magician that hung on one wall. The eyes were bright with an evil glint, and they seemed to follow Petrouchka wherever he turned.

Petrouchka lay sprawled on the floor for a long time. Why should he get up when he had nothing to do?

But he could not lie there forever. After a while he pulled himself to his feet and began to pace about the tiny cell. How terrible to have a human soul locked in the body of a puppet! he thought in despair. Or to have feelings with no way to express them. To be forever imprisoned in this cell!

Petrouchka paced back and forth. But once, as he passed the door, he came to a halt. Perhaps it was unlocked! Perhaps there was hope, after all. Petrouchka's heart beat fast as he reached out to try the knob. It wouldn't budge. He tried again and again, first with one hand, then the other, then both. It was useless.

Driven almost mad, Petrouchka began to bang on the walls. At first he did this out of anger, but when it crossed his mind that someone might hear and come to his rescue, he pounded even harder.

No one heard him, and no one came to his rescue.

At last Petrouchka stopped his banging and sat down, dejected, on the floor. His thoughts wandered to the beautiful Ballerina.

The mere idea of her sent his spirits soaring, and in no time Petrouchka got to his feet and danced a jubilant little dance, right there in his cell. As he did, the door opened and in danced the Ballerina herself! She was just as beautiful as Petrouchka remembered. Her eyelashes were as long, her cheeks as red, her mouth as sweet.

In his excitement, Petrouchka began to show off, hoping to impress his beloved. He jumped up and down, he hopped and bounced and leaped in the air, he whirled and twirled, flinging himself in every direction.

All this time, the Ballerina was looking at him with disdain. She shrugged one beautiful shoulder in disgust and turned away.

Petrouchka was frantic. He leaped higher and higher.

But the Ballerina smothered a yawn and danced over to the door. It opened as if by magic, and she slipped out. When Petrouchka tried to follow her, though, the door slammed in his face. Once more the hopeless, hapless little puppet was locked alone in his wretched cell.

With the slam of the door, Petrouchka sank back into despair. But his despair soon turned to fury and he rushed around the cell, beating his fists against the walls again. Suddenly, he banged so hard that his hand went right through!

At first Petrouchka could only stare at the hole he had made. Slowly he began to realize what this meant. He might be able to escape. And if he did . . . if he did . . .

He would be free. Free from the fairgrounds that he loathed so; free from his hated master; free from this terrible world where no one understood him. Hope surged in Petrouchka's heart. Boldly, he poked his head through the hole and looked out.

There was nothing beyond but darkness.

The hole led nowhere at all.

It was more than Petrouchka could bear. He collapsed on the floor and lay there, sadder and sorrier than ever.

After the Old Magician had thrown Petrouchka into his mean little cell, he had locked the Moor into *his* cell. Like the clown, the Moor was a prisoner. But he was held prisoner in luxurious surroundings.

The room was comfortably furnished, with a couch and soft cushions scattered all about. Now the Moor lolled against them and played with a coconut.

First he tossed it up with his huge hands and caught it with his feet. Then he held it to his ear and shook it. Finally, he tried to break it open and find out what was inside. He threw the coconut to the floor; he slammed it against the ceiling. When that didn't work, he drew his gleaming scimitar and slashed at it with all his might.

But it was useless. Nothing could break the coconut open. The Moor decided that the coconut must be magic. He would worship it! Folding his hands together, he fell to his knees and began to say a strange little prayer. "O coconut," he murmured. "O coconut!"

The Moor was still on his knees when the door to his cell slowly opened. Looking up, he saw the Ballerina standing in the doorway. She began to play a tune on a tiny tin trumpet, and she danced to the music. The Moor was so delighted by her visit that he completely forgot the coconut. Getting to his feet, he began to dance with her.

The two made a curious couple: the tiny, delicate Ballerina and the huge, towering Moor. The Ballerina would have been happy to dance with him forever, but the Moor had another idea. He led her to the couch and tried to pull her down beside him.

The Ballerina shook her head and put her hands up, as if to push the Moor away. But soon she was settled on his lap.

In his dark, cramped cell, far from the richly decorated quarters of the Moor, poor Petrouchka sensed that the Ballerina was in danger. Hurrying to the hole he had punched in the wall earlier, he stuck his head out again. It was dark as midnight, and terrifying to the puppet. But his love was so great that he didn't hesitate at all.

With a mighty effort Petrouchka squeezed through the jagged hole. He felt his way carefully along a passage. When he tripped in the darkness and fell, he picked himself up and went on. At last, at the end of the passage, he came to an opening. He saw a door over to one side. Petrouchka put his shoulder against it, giving a mighty shove. The door opened only slightly, just enough for him to see the two puppets on the couch.

Petrouchka was furious at the sight, and his fury gave him strength. Putting his shoulder to the door again, he gave it another push. This time the door flew open. As it did, the Moor and the Ballerina sprang apart.

By now, Petrouchka was consumed by jealousy. He shook his fist at the Moor and railed at his rival, raging and ranting and fuming.

The Moor was astonished. Was this really Petrouchka, the pathetic little clown? While the puppet raged, the Moor stood with his arms crossed over his brawny chest. He smiled down at Petrouchka, first in amusement, then in scorn. But at last the Moor flew into a rage himself. Drawing his huge scimitar from its place at his side, he lunged at the clown.

Petrouchka tried to run away, but the Moor came after him, chasing him around and around the cell. The Ballerina watched in terror, then let out a bloodcurdling scream. Petrouchka didn't even hear it. He reached the door and squeezed through it, just ahead of the Moor and his terrible sword. He ran right into the square.

Night was falling, but the square was crowded with a host of merrymakers. Many wore strange masks and costumes, abandoning themselves to the spirit of the fair. Gypsies and noblemen alike danced to the music of the hurdy-gurdy, kicking up their heels and whirling about. Storytellers entertained groups of revellers with fantastical tales. People came out to their doorsteps to marvel at the blur of gaiety, excitement, dance and stories and joyous laughter.

Suddenly, though, the festivity was interrupted by a piercing cry from one booth, the Living Theatre at the end of the square. Abruptly all the merrymaking stopped.

The cry echoed through the air as the terrified little Petrouchka dashed into the middle of the square. Close on his heels was the Moor, and close behind the Moor was the panic-stricken Ballerina.

As he ran, the Moor brandished his scimitar. The bedraggled little clown did his best to dodge the blade, and at first it seemed that he might succeed. But he was no match for the Moor, who cornered him with ease.

Quaking with fear, Petrouchka closed his eyes and covered his face with his arms. Once . . . twice . . . three times, the arrogant Moor whirled his scimitar over his head. Then, with a great cry and a mighty lunge, he brought it crashing down on Petrouchka.

The little puppet gave a single cry and fell to the ground. His tiny body quivered. Then the quivering stopped. Petrouchka was dead.

The crowd was horrified. As the shock wore off, sadness took its place. A small boy picked up Petrouchka's lifeless arm, and a tear ran down his cheek. An old peasant woman, a babushka, crossed herself. Two Gypsies shook their heads sorrowfully and whispered to one another. Petrouchka's death seemed so real that no one believed he was only a puppet.

Finally someone sent for a policeman, who came rushing up with the Old Magician. "What's this? What has happened?" the Old Magician demanded.

When he had heard the story, the Old Magician laughed. "A murder?" he said. "A murder? But Petrouchka is only a doll!" Laughing still, he picked Petrouchka up by his collar and held him out for the crowd to see. "He's only a puppet," the Old Magician told them. "A doll stuffed with straw!"

Then he started back towards his booth, dragging Petrouchka behind him.

As he walked, the Old Magician began to hear some faint music. It was the little tune he had played for Petrouchka when he danced. Now, looking up, the Old Magician saw Petrouchka himself, standing on the roof of the theatre.

This was the real Petrouchka, the Petrouchka with a heart and soul. It was the Petrouchka who loved the Ballerina dearly—and who hated the Old Magician just as passionately. A few flakes of snow fluttered down, and Petrouchka caught one on his tongue, as he had always longed to do. Now he was free to savour the biting cold. When spring came, he would be free to smell flowers, to bask in the warmth of the sun. It was the freedom he had always dreamed about.

Looking down to the square, he saw the Old Magician standing there, holding the body of the puppet. The real Petrouchka waved to the man who had been his master. "What I said is true," his wave seemed to say. "I really do have a soul."

Suddenly the Old Magician grew frightened. The little clown, he realized, had indeed been murdered!

By now, the square was almost deserted. As the sky began to brighten with the new day, the *blini* lady was closing up her stall. The one who tended the samovar was taking off her apron, getting ready to leave. But the Old Magician kept gazing upward.

His thoughts still on spring, Petrouchka waved again.

A deep, sad sigh escaped the Old Magician's lips. Shaking his head, he started slowly towards his booth once more, dragging the puppet behind him. It was as limp as a rag, with straw stuffing spilling out where the Moor had slashed it. Again the Old Magician heard Petrouchka's tune. Now it sounded like a funeral march, and he knew it would haunt him forever.

Above the square the other, the real, Petrouchka watched him. Triumphantly, he waved one last time to the Old Magician.

To Shirley, who made books like this possible – J.C.

To Donnie — V.W.

Originally published in the U.S.A. 1992
by Viking Penguin Inc., New York, a division of
Penguin Books U.S.A., Inc.
First published in Great Britain 1992
by Victor Gollancz Ltd.
14 Henrietta Street, London WC2E 8QJ

A catalogue record for this book is available from
the British Library

ISBN 0 575 05477 8

Printed in Singapore